EDGES

Rousing Attack

Book 2

Bjorn Esterday Was Not Born Yesterday

Wynter Sommers

GJ dePillis

TXu001885818
PAu 3-627-478, 1-798104171, PAu003401882, PAu003759141,
1-787-353831
Library of Congress Control Number: 2019930920

Published by Pure Force Enterprises, Inc.
California, USA
Since 2002

INGRAM

INGRAM® Distribution

ISBN-13:978-1-7184-0003-0
ISBN-10: 1-7184-0003-9

DEDICATION

To all of us whose hearts reach out to change the world around, whose minds calculate the next strategic move, whose souls crave adventure and value freedom of democracy. To the spirit harnessing the power of fiction to alter our reality, making the world a better place for everyone.

Bjorn Esterday Was Not Born Yesterday Series

Firebrand (9 Stories +Lesson Plan Book)
Edges (9 Stories +Lesson Plan Book)
Gone (18 Stories + 2 Lesson Plan Books)

Bjorn EDGES Series
EDGES Book 1-Swift Encounter
EDGES Book 2-Rousing Attack
EDGES Book 3-One Foot Under
EDGES Book 4-Earthshake
EDGES Book 5-Broken String
EDGES Book 6-Key Witness
EDGES Book 7-Who is She?
EDGES Book 8-Vanish
EDGES Book 9-Chase or Die

Bjorn Series Alternate Reading Plan

1st   Edges Book 1
2nd   Edges Book 2
3rd   Gone Book 1
4th   Firebrand Book 1
5th   Edges Book 3
6th   Firebrand Book 2
7th   Gone Book 2
8th   Gone Book 3
9th   Firebrand Book 3
10th   Gone Book 4
11th   Firebrand Book 4
12th   Gone Book 5
13th   Gone Book 6
14th   Edges Book 4
15th   Firebrand Book 5
16th   Gone Book 7
17th   Firebrand Book 6
18th   Gone Book 8
19th   Firebrand Book 7
20th   Gone Book 9
21st   Firebrand Book 8
22nd   Gone Book 10
23rd   Gone Book 11
24th   Gone Book 12
25th   Gone Book 13
26th   Firebrand Book 9 (End)
27th   Gone Book 14
28th   Gone Book 15
29th   Gone Book 16
30th   Gone Book 17
31st   Gone Book 18 (End)
32nd   Edges Book 5
33rd   Edges Book 6
34th   Edges Book 7
35th   Edges Book 8
36th   Edges Book 9 (End)

Main Characters

- **Sarah Paradise** - School Teacher
- **Bjorn Esterday** - Reporter at the Daily Memo Newspaper. Works for Sammy Scribe.
- **Percy Snatcher** - Head of the AnCor para-military cell
- **Slash** - Loyal AnCor follower of Percy
- **Noah Lantz** - Earth Farmer husband to Ruth Lantz
- **Joshua Lantz** - Earth Farmer child of Ruth and Noah Lantz
- **Ruth Lantz** - Earth Farmer Mother to Joshua. Wife to Noah. Expert quilter.
- **Jack Courtly** - Head of Courtly City
- **Queenie Courtly** -Wife to Jack Courtly
- **Ace Courtly** - Child of Jack and Queenie Courtly
- **Skipper Courtly** - Brother to Jack Courtly
- **Pip Courtly** - Child of Skipper Courtly
- **Widow Medicina**- Courtly City citizen and train passenger, recently widowed.
- **Mrs Libris** - Librarian

Characters (continued)

- **Train** passengers
- **Soldier** Police
- **Soldier Police Officer** Gene
- **AntiCorporatists** aka AnCors
- **Library** patrons
- **Sammy Scribe** Bjorn's editor
- **Workers** at Courtly mail office
- **Summer students** at Courtly Offices

CONTENTS

ACKNOWLEDGMENTS

To all those gentle souls who have graciously given tokens of love, hope, and kind considerations to others.

0 Preface

Previously, we witnessed that Slash, the AnCor,was being hunted by the Soldier Police of Courtly City at the train station.

Bjorn had scooped up Sarah Paradise on horseback and rode to Library so she could meet her small students and give them lessons in how to read a paper book. But, will Mrs. Libris, the librarian at Library, be able to convincc Sarah's students about the value of truth and learning facts?

Will Sarah ever see investigative reporter, Bjorn Esterday, again?

1 CHAPTER Year 2030: Game Locked Away (Continuous Ch 13)

The train became noisier as it picked up speed.

Even with the Anti-Corporate Activity ACA still in effect, the presence of the Courtly family was enough to allow that train to move on schedule.

In the luxurious Courtly cabin, Jack placed his briefcase next to him on the supple leather seat and opened it.

He turned to Ace and muttered, "Courtly Dynamics helps those less fortunate. That's what our company does.

In fact, that's what your mother does with those Earth Farmer quilts. That's what we Courtlys have done for generations."

"Right, Dad, so great grandfather pounced on this town when it declared bankruptcy decades ago," Ace sneered.

"Ace, he didn't pounce. He helped the community by buying up all the old city and county services and other 'distressed businesses'"

"And making us the biggest gorilla around," Ace mocked.

"Ace, you may not agree with everything great grandfather did. Great grandfather just took advantage of an opportunity created by corrupt city officials who mismanaged their own charges. Many other corporations did exactly the same thing when cities began declaring bankruptcy." Jack shook his head, realizing his child was missing the point. "Ace, Look at your mother. Model her example, her kindness."

"Nobles Oblige? Yeah, I've heard this

one before," Ace retorted.

"Listen!" Jack snapped, "A Courtly is never rude. Understand?"

Ace, still defiant, whispered, "Sewing anything by hand is so slow...so stupid...what's the point?"

Queenie felt useless in things like this. Disciplining children was really for nannies and such. But she felt lucky her husband had decided to manage some of those tasks. She, however, took pride in the favors she doled out to others, thereby creating jobs for the less fortunate.

Her husband was unusual in that he sometimes chose to tackle difficult problems head on, such as teaching manners to Ace. Queenie was confident that demonstrating kindness to a lost widow taking heart pills in the corridor, for example, would satisfy her role, always on display for the general populace, as perfect model-parent. It did, after all, take two parents to raise a child. Queenie wondered if Aces' eagerness to aggressively challenge everything would ever be tempered.

She turned toward Ace and Jack, satisfied with her good deed.

"There," Queenie smiled, "now we can get reacquainted as a family. Ace, did you see how a Courtly speaks to a less fortunate soul? Do you understand why I spoke to that stranger and freely offered her our chilled hydration?"

Ace reached into Mr. Courtly's briefcase and scooped up the electronic device, becoming absorbed in the hand held game. Without looking up from the hypnotic screen, Ace replied, "Yeah,yeah, Noblesse Oblige...still don't care..."

Jack deftly removed the device from the youth's hands and smoothly popped it back into his briefcase, locking the heavy gold latches silently into place. Jack inhaled slowly, as one does when one must embark on an odious task.

Turning toward the shaft of sunlight streaming through their compartment window, Queenie sighed as she eased herself down onto a plump, softly overstuffed leather chair. She popped open her gold filigree jeweled compact to check on her appearance. She did not wish to appear curious, but she also wanted a distraction since she wondered how Ace would react to what Jack was about to say

2 CHAPTER Year 2030: Ace Gets Sassy (Continuous Ch 14)

As expected, Ace started to protest, "Dad, I was almost at the next level and you..."

Jack interrupted. Queenie knew he would.

"Ace! Stop whining about that game. It will stay locked away!"

"Dad. I can't stand it! Everything is so boring!" Ace whined.

"You are a Courtly. The Courtly family always works hard. But, the Courtly family is still a family. We are taking

6

this trip, without any staff this time, because your mother's therapist said we need to bond without distractions. No games. Not even servants."

Ace groaned.

Queenie snapped shut her compact mirror as if about to speak, but remained silent and simply observed.

"Dad..." Ace's eyes rolled, refusing to absorb any correction.

"Don't 'Dad...' me. Your Uncle Skipper has raised your cousin Pip to be a self-centered sponge." Jack continued, now noticing that Ace was looking satisfied that cousin Pip was actually being called out for the bully he really was.

Jack continued, "Although your uncle Skipper is my brother, that part of the family, I'm very sad to say, tarnishes the Courtly name. We all have a choice about how we react to the circumstances life gives us."

Jack inhaled before proceeding.

"Your behavior, Ace, at that

7

VanDeMark Academy...your fifth school transfer, may I remind you, was inexcusable. I'd rather have you emulate those honest God-fearing Earth Farmers than copy any habits or behaviors from Pip or Uncle Skipper. But, the fact is they are still family and I must show even them kindness."

Just outside the private Courtly car, Percy Snatcher silently maneuvered to peek inside the door window, unnoticed. Percy pulled out the sweat-crumpled newspaper and studied the photograph in his palm, then at the profile of a man inside the cabin with his clean little family. Percy was satisfied he had just identified the right target and then left.

It was not yet time to strike.

Meanwhile, inside the cabin, Ace pleaded with both parents.

"Look, I just got into a little trouble at some stupid school. I don't know why you wouldn't work with that judge..."

Jack snapped, "You mean bribe the judge to reduce your punishment like

Uncle Skipper did for Pip?"

"Yes, Dad, yes. Yes. Yes. Yes!" Ace defiantly crossed both arms. "You are so completely over-reacting about this. All I want to do is be left alone with my game and get to the next level so I won't be bored on this stupid train with this stupid family vacation idea. So stupid! Nobody understands how hard my life is and all the stupid things I have to deal with."

Ace spoke triumphantly and reached for the brief case, starting to fiddle with the elegant golden latches.

Jack snapped back, "You know that prototype is not a toy. That will stay in my briefcase for the rest of this journey."

Jack's jaw clenched as he jerked his briefcase from Ace's grasp, firmly placing it by the cabin door.

"Then, I guess I'll just be bored on this stupid trip!" Ace turned away in the seat, eyes closed, chin jutting out, shutting off both parents to emphasize the sacrifice Ace was making, here.

Jack looked at Queenie and with only a glance, Queenie gave her consent for Jack to do what would happen next.

3 CHAPTER Year 2030: Meet The Lantz family (Continuous Ch 15)

While gripping the arm of his squirming child, Jack Courtly rapped on the third class cabin door. The door opened to reveal an Earth Farmer woman, wearing their traditional dark blue long dress. Her hair was up in a bun modestly covered by a simple bonnet. She smiled warmly and said, "Yes, may we help you?" She held a quilt square that she had been sewing.

Her husband was reading what looked to be the Bible, and the son, about age 14, was reading another book. They both glanced up at their visitors.

11

Ace's eyes rolled as Jack Courtly dragged Ace inside the cramped train compartment of the Lantz family.

The train was making a rhythmic hum as it zipped along the tracks.

Jack introduced himself, "Hello. I'm Jack Courtly. My wife, Queenie, says you are working on a quilt for Ace, here."

As soon as they heard the Courtly name, the entire Lantz family stood in deference.

The woman said, "Oh, for Mrs. Courtly! You must be little Ace." She smiled at Ace.

Jack continued, "My wife said you had a child about Ace's age and thought they may get along during the train ride."

Ace tried desperately to avoid eye contact with everyone.

"I am Noah Lantz, husband of Ruth, father to Joshua." Noah formally bowed. His wife gave a deep curtsy. Noah shot a look at his son, who quickly also bowed.

Jack gave the signal to be relaxed and motioned his permission for the family to sit.

"Greetings, Mr. Courtly," Ruth Lantz smiled at Jack and then turned to Ace. "And it's nice to meet you, as well, Little Ace. I'm sewing your mommy's design for your quilt right now." Ruth produced two quilting squares not yet attached to each other and showed it to Ace.

Already bored, Ace looked out the dusty small window and gazed into the azure blue sky, which was dotted with festive colorful hot air balloons languidly floating above. A bright sunbeam streamed into the cabin, past Ace, illuminating the fabric creations. The morning fog had burned away to reveal a lovely afternoon.

Oblivious to manners, Ace turned back toward the Lantz family and looked at the two twelve inch squares of fabric, and snapped, "That's supposed to keep me warm? It's really small."

Ruth stifled a good-natured chuckle. She explained that by stitching the two

13

squares together, it would form a larger new design. She demonstrated with swift expert stitches.

Ruth continued, patting the hard plank bench on which they all sat, inviting Ace to sit next to her. "There are several women in our community who have worked on different pieces of this quilt. After we complete sewing the top, then we stitch it together to make all the edges fit perfectly...like a solved jigsaw puzzle."

Noah spoke to Jack while Ruth explained to Ace how a quilt was constructed.

"Mr. Courtly, we cannot offer the amusements Ace may be used to, but your wife has been very kind to my wife. Ace is most welcomed to be our guest and work on puzzles or read a book with our son, Joshua, while we are aboard this train, if you so wish it, Sir."

Ace, overhearing this exchange, looked horrified at Jack, dreading a parental response.

Jack smiled broadly. "Great idea. Thank you, Mr. Lantz." Jack promptly left the cabin, leaving Ace behind with the Lantz family.

Ace's voice trembled, "Dad?"

4 CHAPTER Year 2030: Jack Arranges A Nice Dinner (Continuous Ch 16)

As Jack stepped back into the ornate Courtly cabin, Mrs. Queenie Courtly, relieved, showed him two hats and asked him, "This one is a cool dove-grey sand shade, while that one is a warm sunrise caramel...Which one should I wear tomorrow?"

Jack smiled as he grabbed Queenie, kissing her, "I see you are missing your personal assistant."

"She makes selecting an outfit seem so easy. It's a little frustrating that I can't contact her for her guidance on my outfit because we are trying to limit using electronics around Ace. Jack, do you think that when we get there we could summon at least one of my assistants?" Queenie asked hopefully.

Jack shook his head, "...and violate the guidelines your therapist laid out for us to bond as a family?"

She reached up to kiss Jack's cheek. He welcomed the warm affections of his wife.

"So," Queenie cooed, "is Ace thoroughly occupied interacting with humans instead of hiding in silly games?" She kissed him softly on his neck.

Slowly, Jack rubbed his wife's shoulders and back. Queenie reacted to her husband's electric touch.

"Jack, Ace isn't going to get fed up with the Lantz family and come barging in on us, hmmm?"

Jack wrapped a loving arm around her as he pulled Queenie down onto the sofa.

He gently kissed his wife. The feel of her soft cheek against his while he inhaled her custom-blended perfume was always welcomed at the end of a harsh work-day. Her touch soothed, yet excited him. It felt good to be alone with his wife.

Queenie melted, mesmerized by his caresses. Her lips searched for his. Jack's eyes opened and spied his own briefcase by the door.

Suddenly, he stood up.

"To keep Ace-Our-Little-Terror with the Lantz family, I need to do something," Jack smiled.

Queenie produced a handkerchief and wiped some red lipstick from Jack's mouth as she asked, "Oh? And what is that?"

"I'm off to ask chef to create a gourmet meal for dinner for all of us. Queenie, I know it's in the opposite direction, but would you mind going down to the Lantz cabin and invite them to join us for dinner while I get to the dining car to make sure the bill comes to me. And remember, they might not let them into the private dining car unless you accompany them. Maybe if they are well fed, Ruth and Noah would keep Ace all night and give us some privacy after dinner..."

"...to...continue where we left off, Darling?" Queenie helpfully added with a flirtatious glance.

Jack gave his blushing bride a quick kiss and headed toward the dining car, threading his way through other passengers walking in that same direction.

Queenie reapplied her lipstick, snapped her expensive compact shut when satisfied that she looked flawless, then made her way down to the Lantz family third class car. Queenie looked forward to personally escorting them to a gourmet dinner treat.

As Jack strode toward the dining car, his mind was clouded with thoughts of Ace. Jack wondered if his motives were really to thank the Lantz family or if it was to get rid of Ace for an evening. He

19

wondered if this dinner would change his feelings about his own child. Or, would his child finally learn to appreciate the life Courtly Corp had provided?

Jack inadvertently bumped into Percy, who was just donning a white waiter jacket. Percy froze with his jacket half on. The crumpled newspaper photo floated to the ground. Always a gentleman, Jack, not realizing it was a photograph of himself, handed it absentmindedly to Percy and kept walking. Percy accepted the photo while continuing to slip his jacket on as he stared at the back of Jack's retreating form.

Another waiter, also clad in a white serving jacket, came up behind Percy, handing him a pitcher of water. "Could you head to 2nd class cabins and make sure the guests have hydration?"

5 CHAPTER- Year 2030: Where Is Ace? (Continuous Ch 17)

Farmer's wife, Ruth Lantz, her arms straining to hold onto a large cloth sewing bag with all her supplies, followed Queenie Courtly who was burdened with carrying just her small cabin key. They walked together down a long corridor toward the dining car. Ruth excitedly chatted with Queenie about the same two quilting squares that Ruth had shown Ace earlier.

Queenie, pleased with the way the design was turning out, placed the soft cotton against her check as she felt the comfort of the luxurious thread-count in the sateens and jacquards.

"The weft and warp of this fabric is so

21

fine and unexpectedly soft and the hand- or feel- of the fabric is marvelous. The patterns are beautiful. I'm so happy you were able to find these cottons in the colors I selected, Ruth. I'm thrilled that my design is coming to fruition! I feel so useful, now. Positively entrepreneurial, darling."

The two youths, Ace and Joshua both trailed behind.

"I'm so pleased you like the way it's coming along, Mrs. Courtly," Ruth beamed. "Your design is creative. I have not made one like this before, but I think it will turn out fine."

"Oh better than fine, Ruth. Our creation will be a masterpiece. Something to display in a museum. Your skills and expert craftsmanship have given me the opportunity to be creative. Between us, we will make Ace a stunning heirloom, which will be handed down to future generations."

"We hope it will be satisfactory, Mrs. Courtly. We are thankful for all you've done for our village."

"Now, tell me, again, Ruth, why is your husband in the 1st class dining car?" chirped Queenie. "I got distracted when you first mentioned it."

Ruth replied, "Certainly. There is no other dining car on the train, save for first class. We only packed enough food for the three of us, so Mr. Lantz went to fetch soup and crackers for Ace's dinner tonight." Ruth Lantz smiled, hoping Queenie would understand.

"Oh, goodness. I've forgotten people pack their food before a trip. No, darling. Forget your soup and crackers. You and Noah and Joshua are our guests for dinner. Tonight you dine with us! Jack is arranging things with the executive chef as we speak. You should not be expected to use your credits to feed Ace."

"This is all very kind of you," Ruth smiled and looked back at her son Joshua still walking in glum silence beside Ace. "Won't papa be very surprised?" Then, Ruth turned back to Queenie alarmed, "Oh, I'm afraid I'm not dressed for your first class dining car."

"Fiddlesticks. You look delightful. We love your costumes."

Ruth smiled at her son Joshua and added "Well, I don't think Joshua has ever eaten in a dining car before. Have you, my child?"

Joshua softly replied, "No, Ma'am."

Queenie turned to look at Ace, then glanced at the public restroom they were passing in the hallway, then back at Ace.

Ace grumbled to Joshua, "I think we need to wash our hands before we go into the dining car, Joshua."

"Ok."

"But, I'll race you, Joshua... to that washroom over there." The adolescent giggles were tuned out by the mothers as Ace started to run. Ace slowed down and let Joshua gain a length or two.

Joshua nearly collided with Percy Snatcher, now dressed in a waiter's jacket as he emerged from the 2nd class cabins after stashing the water pitcher away into a closet.

Percy urgently made his way along the aisle, frustrated that his path was blocked by the passengers slowly strolling ahead of him. Percy shoved past Joshua and then impatiently stepped ahead of the two women, Ruth and Queenie.

As he hurried along toward the 1st class dining car, Queenie, watched him go, suppressing that twinge of anxiety which happens when something is amiss, but you just don't know why.

With the mothers' backs turned, and Joshua now in the restroom, Ace passed the Courtly compartment, unlocked the door with the spare key, and grabbed Dad's briefcase. Shaking it, to make sure the toy was still inside, Ace tried quickly to unlock the briefcase, but couldn't. Then, holding the brief case, Ace slipped out of the Courtly private cabin and hid the briefcase in a hallway slot near the exit. Ace planned to figure out how to pop open Dad's secure golden latches later.

Almost as soon as Ace had finished

tucking the briefcase away, Joshua emerged from the restroom.

Their mothers, still walking toward the dining car, were much farther ahead.

Joshua quickly caught up to his mother.

Meanwhile, Ace hurried into the empty washroom, closed the door and turned on the water, passing both hands underneath the stream, then shook droplets off. Ace opened the door, or at least tried to.

Sometimes these doors stick, Ace recalled, fiddling with the door handle and lock, then pressing against the door.

The door was stuck. Ace was trapped inside.

In the hallway, Queenie turned around seeing only Joshua.

"Joshua, do you know where Ace is?"

Joshua looked behind him, but Ace was not in sight.

6 CHAPTER Year 2030: One Exit Blocked (Continuous Ch 18)

Rich velvet brocade curtains in the first class dining car were closed to keep out the bright late afternoon sun. Highly polished burled wood inlaid paneling gleamed against shiny brass accents. Soothing music played in the background. The tables were small, but looked inviting with crisp white tablecloths and fresh flowers in crystal vases anchored to the wall by well-polished sconces.

Everything about the dining area conveyed peace, elegance, and promises of a deliciously memorable meal.

One dining passenger was absorbed in his newspaper. The front-page headline read: "Civil Unrest- Anti-Corporatists vs. Our Patriotic Soldier Police".

A smaller story was titled: "Increased Earthshake Activity".

Percy Snatcher, wearing his white waiter's jacket, jammed a thin piece of metal into the door lock, making it stick. Now, he just had one more door to barricade on the other side of the dining car. His eyes darted about evaluating the 1st class patrons.

Noah Lantz, at the far end of the dining car, was trying to complete his food purchase with an impatient maitre d'.

Jack Courtly emerged from the chef's kitchen, clearly satisfied with the arrangements he had made.

Jack was pleased when he spotted Noah, yet Noah, being absorbed with the transaction for biscuits had not yet seen Jack.

Jack started to approach Noah to show

him where dinner would be served, so Jack didn't see Percy jump up and dash toward Noah.

Jack didn't see that through the ornate windows, outside there were old dusty trucks, cars and vans driving alongside to keep pace with the train.

Jack didn't see that each jalopy was packed with adrenaline pumped Anti-Corporatists, or AnCors. With the insulated train and soothing background music, Jack didn't hear the angry vehement shouts outside.

Nobody in the dining car saw the people outside, except for Percy.

They were too early.

No time to block the second exit.

7 CHAPTER Year 2030: AnCors On Board (Continuous Ch 19)

Percy targeted Noah because he was an Earth Farmer and on the protected list. They were an endangered species. Courtly charities raised money to protect the Earth Farmers and set up commerce agreements with them. Lavish galas were thrown to raise money to support their ridiculous way of life: building paths for their horses, promising to let them buy land with clean soil to farm on, promising to stock city grocery markets with their farmed fresh produce instead of the simulated foods, which had a much longer shelf life. The thought of supporting these Earthies disgusted

Percy.

Percy shoved his only gun into Noah's ribs. Jack was horrified.

"I've no quarrel with you, brother," Noah simply stated to the gunman.

Jack tried to reason with Percy, "Earth Farmers don't believe in violence, Sir."

The diners froze.

The man with the newspaper glanced at a photograph in the paper, looked up at Jack Courtly, then again at the paper, and immediately rushed out the back exit, leaving his paper behind. Percy couldn't afford to waste a bullet, and let him go. AnCor comrades would deal with him later, anyway.

On exiting, the man nearly collided with a Soldier Police entering the dining car. His name badge, read "Gene". Percy used the badge as a target and fired. The wounded SP grunted and was thrown back against the wall, blood pouring from his head. Police Soldier Gene hit an electronic button on his uniform,

31

then fell to the ground and lay motionless, leaving a vertical smear of blood on the walnut paneling.

The report of gunfire caused one patron to drop his monocle, which splashed into his tea cup. Another patron fainted from the sudden sound, sliding out of his chair, pulling the tablecloth with him. Another stood up abruptly, sending his full plate of noodles and sauce onto the young woman he had earlier introduced disingenuously as his "niece".

Percy glanced quickly at the dusty vehicles still keeping pace with the train outside.

The train was still moving too fast. Why wasn't the train slowing down?

Percy found his voice, which cracked at first from not having water, then became a hoarse angry blast, "Our cause needs money. Who will make a donation to our cause?"

Jack, now the closest to Percy and Noah, calmly stated, "That hostage you are holding has no money. Let him go."

Grabbing Noah even tighter, Percy breathed a pungent fume of words into Noah's ear, "Make a donation to my cause."

Noah had only the change from the snacks he had just purchased. He dropped his coins into Percy's palm. This infuriated Percy and he took a step back to fully aim at Noah and cocked the gun.

"With all the free handouts you Earthies get from these rich idiots, you should have more money than this!" Percy seethed.

Jack lunged for the emergency cord, which brought the train to a screeching halt, throwing Percy off balance. The dead stop tossed everybody out of their seats. Objects flew. Some passengers were slammed to the floor and knocked unconscious.

Jack shouted at Noah, "Run! Get your family off this train!" as Jack stumbled toward Percy, grabbing for the gun.

Instantly, Noah turned his back to obey Jack, and sought escape.

Percy's gun went off again.

Jack felt a sting, then nothing but a mix of cold and heat tingling, then going numb. He measured his breathing to try and stay conscious. He saw the white crisp tablecloth before him dot with drops of his own blood. Jack felt weak, but still forced himself to fight as if his arms and legs could follow orders even if he couldn't feel them anymore.

Noah raced to the dining compartment exit, but the door was stuck...or locked...

The struggle between Percy and Jack continued as the gun fired again.

Immediately, as the train stopped, the Anti-Corporatist vehicles outside also screeched to a halt, flanking the first class area. Out tumbled angry, sweaty men from their old rusting vehicles patched up from a by-gone era. Enraged Anti-Corporatists AnCors armed with a mix of archaic and modern weapons, raced with victorious shouts to board the train.

It was theirs, now.

8 CHAPTER Year 2030: No Way, Lady (Continuous Ch 20)

Queenie Courtly and Ruth Lantz approached the dining car door. Ace finally got that rest room door opened and raced to catch up to Joshua who excitedly pointed that Ace was right there.

The women looked.

Queenie was relieved. "Stay near me, Ace. I know you say I get over cautious, but I'd just feel better knowing you were nearby."

Ace just smirked. "Whatever, Mom."

The tiny round port-hole window in the dining car door was almost within view when suddenly the two women and both children were thrown against the walls of the narrow train corridor.

Ruth's oversized bag fell off her shoulder and she crouched to collect her things for the second time that day.

"Was that an Earthshake?" Queenie gasped, "Did you hear something odd?"

Ruth just shrugged as she dragged her bag back onto her shoulder. Ruth now approached the dining car door and looked through the window. Alarmed, she grabbed Queenie's arm.

"That man," Ruth gasped, "That waiter is attacking your husband, Mrs. Courtly!"

Confused and stunned, Queenie stammered disbelieving, "Jack?"

Noah's panicked face suddenly appeared through the porthole window of the dining car door. Noah's attempts to open the door became frantic as Ruth struggled to loosen the lock on her side. Noah motioned for her to back away.

Ruth spun around to Ace and got eye level, "Ace, I know this is a nice new jacket, but it's too fancy. You are safer without it."

Ace snapped back, "No way, lady!"

Queenie also turned to Ace, "Baby, your daddy's been hurt. He needs my help. Go with Mrs. Latnz. We will come to get you when we can. Your daddy and I love you."

Ace, perplexed, defiantly said, "Mom! You can't be serious."

Queenie, now absorbing the gravity of the situation sternly said, "No time, Baby Ace. Remember your prayers and go!"

At that moment more shots were heard. The door sprang open. Noah tumbled through.

Ruth, relieved to see her husband was not hurt, sharply stated, "Mrs. Courtly wants us to take Ace with us. She wants to stay here."

Noah took one deep breath as they all ran toward the hallway exit, "Mrs. Courtly, your husband – Jack Courtly – He saved my life. Thank him for me, please. But, if you insist on staying, hide in this closet. Now."

"Hide?"

Noah opened the corridor closet door and pushed Queenie inside, slamming it shut with her firmly hidden.

Queenie found she just barely fit. She was tortured by images of her bloodied husband needing help.

After a moment of dead silence, Queenie heard the heavy disorganized footsteps and angry shouts of Anti-Corporatists boarding the train, cheering victoriously. Then a spray of bullets and more cheers. It sounded as if they were playing a game and giving out points for people shot.

The Lantz family ran, dragging Ace with them.

9 CHAPTER Year 2030: Find the Woman (Continuous Ch 21)

The once pristine dining car was now a desperate scene of blood and chaos. Percy stood to wave triumphantly as he opened the door allowing others from his clan to start rounding up living passengers. Next to him, on the floor, the trampled blood splattered newspaper was still opened to the society pages.

Percy noticed it under his feet. As he looked down, he saw a large photo of Mr. and Mrs. Courtly smiling at some gala fundraiser. He picked up the soggy sheet and read a portion of the story out loud.

"Jack Courtly, C.E.O., believes he is obligated to set an example for the corporation by taking a family vacation. The leader sets the tone. If you love your family, they will support you in your dream-job. I love my family and before I take this vacation, I am authorizing increased holiday hours across the board for all Courtly staff so they can spend more time with their families and return to work energized to give Courtly Dynamics Corporation 110%!"

Percy ripped the picture out of the newspaper disgusted as he stepped over the motionless Soldier Police Guard Gene to meet with a boarding AnCor as other AnCors were ushering off ambulatory survivors.

"Mr. Snatcher, I was told you wanted to see me?" The AnCor stood by awaiting orders.

Percy whipped out the crumpled photo, blood partially obscuring the image. He then pointed to the collapsed heap of Jack Courtly across the dining car.

"This man had a wife. She is here

somewhcre. I might collect a ransom for her. For our cause. Find her."

Percy shoved the photograph into the AnCor's hand, who, without question, turned and raced off to execute his orders.

10 CHAPTER Year 2036: Executive Headquarters (Continuous Ch 22)

Six years later: 2036.

Streams of employees poured through early morning fog into the lobby of executive headquarters. A muted sun glowed behind the misty sky as it cast a shadow-less blush of sunlight on the formal gardens of the Courtly Dynamics Corporation campus.

Birds chirped as they flew and nestled in the nooks and crannies of trees. As they flew, their muted shadows slid across the cold, black, geometric panels which absorbed sunlight to provide an unceasing source of energy day and night to office buildings, which soared seventy stories to the sky.

Inside the lobby, the slick polished black stone reception desk fronted a ten foot long exotic fish aquarium. Each visitor entering the lobby was scanned by a light beam which signaled if the individual would be admitted or escorted away by a security detail. Those admitted would check for directions at the reception desk. New visitors were given the aid of a small map drone to escort them to their destination.

Employees were greeted by name and permitted to continue walking in the opposite direction to their work pods.

The spacious corner executive office was decorated with shelves of management affirmation art, as well as hand-blown glass accents. In the oversized ergonomic massage chair sat a 20 year old man, adjusting his glasses to read something in the newspaper. He didn't seem to care much for the cover story, titled "Peace Talks with Anti-Corporatists Collapse". Rather, his attention was drawn to a more colorful distraction on page 3.

"May I enter, Sir?" came a feminine voice through the speaker on the desk.

"Of course," grinned the young man.

In walked Sarah Paradise holding a tray with morning coffee and freshly baked snacks, setting it on his expansive empty desktop. Excited to partake of these goodies, Pip Courtly tore out the comedic image section then tossed the rest of his newspaper to the floor. He now had a new distraction to entertain his short attention span.

Sarah stepped to the discarded newspaper to glance at the headline and only looked up at the young man when he addressed her.

"Who are you?" he demanded, grinning. He slurped his coffee as if he had never eaten in public before. Pastry crumbs cascaded like snowflakes onto his shirt.

"Well, Mr. Courtly, when your secretary went on maternity leave, the agency called me and asked if I would fill in during my mandatory Summer Break from high school."

"You're a high school student?" His grin slid into a leer.

"No. I am an instructor," she corrected. "This is a temporary assignment. But, I've heard that executive headquarters are rich with physical files of newspaper history, so I'm looking forward to spending my summer here examining them." She smiled, hoping he would appreciate her enthusiasm and then dismiss her.

Sarah didn't really want to work at a large office, but she needed income during the summer when she was not paid at all by the school. All her coworkers did something different to earn money during the summer.

"You called me 'Mr. Courtly'? Oh that is funny. Naw. Call me Pip. So...so...so... this is your summer hobby. That's nice. Sarah...I can call you that, right? Sarah, my hobbies are more artistic. Did you know that?" He smiled as he gestured

45

toward his shelves, cluttered with various glass objects.

He examined Sarah Paradise with a gaze that seemed almost tactile to her, starting with her toes, ending with her face. She fidgeted uncomfortably, trying to figure out the best way to excuse herself and get on with earning a paycheck.

Pip Courtly jutted his chin to point in the direction of a small door to one side of the office.

"See that door? It's a work room right behind this place. I blow glass in there. Very private. Want to see?"

Before Sarah could reply, Pip went on, changing the subject abruptly without notice, causing Sarah to struggle for words.

"You know", Sarah started, "realizing how formal this environment is, I'm completely comfortable with calling you Mr. Courtly and you calling me Miss Paradise. I wouldn't want to..."

"Well, Sarah", Pip interrupted, "This is a corporation. Not a school. I'm surprised the schools have enough credits to pay for teachers during the summer sessions."

"They don't, Sir. Education Staff is not paid during the summer. Funding has been reduced again this year, as well, for supplies and salaries. That's why I feel fortunate that I have this job otherwise I wouldn't have any income over the summer."

"Oh, good."

"Good, Mr. Courtly? I don't understand."

"Well, Dad...that's Mr. Skipper Courtly to you, directed the courts to cut all summer funding to schools. I never follow up on these things but I'm glad it kicked in."

"Cut funding? Why?"

"Well, how would Dad say it?" Pip adopted a deeper voice as he mimicked Skipper Courtly, "...We can now give

47

young students that rare opportunity to work in a real business environment. They must log in their unpaid hours in order to graduate. After that, they have the privilege of working with us for an obligatory three additional years for free room and board. And we won't even charge them for this experience." Pip smiled as he continued in his regular voice, "Yup. Sometimes my old man can come up with a clever plan." Pip put his feet up on the desk, satisfied.

For a moment, Sarah stood motionless as she absorbed the fact that her livelihood was impacted because a corporation wanted a legal way to secure slave labor and call it "experience". She had always thought a structured educational work program that paid the students was a better way to prepare young adults for careers and even to learn how to manage money. Sarah Paradise remained speechless.

He looked at her, wondering when she was going to react.

Sarah, poker faced, reasoned she

needed credits to pay bills. Doing this job is all she can afford to focus on right now. She didn't have it in her to crusade for changing society at the moment. She was in no position to challenge her new boss.

"I see. Is there anything else I can get for you Mr. Courtly?"

"Yes. Call me Pip." He smiled looking over his glasses.

At this point, Sarah felt cornered. "All right. Mister...Pip... Pip it is, then." Sarah smiled quickly then pivoted efficiently and left the room, leaving Pip to enjoy his comedic images and crumb-spewing baked treats while laughing with his mouth opened.

He called after her, "Sarah, do you think you will like it here so much that you'll quit working at the school?"

11 CHAPTER Year 2036: New Summer Job (Continuous Ch 23)

Sarah tip-toed through the old Library. She smiled at Mrs. Libris, still there manning her post, ageless, always quiet, and charmingly professional.

Sarah noticed there were, scattered about, a few more people visiting Library than had been in years past.

She recalled that one moment, that gently defiant choice she had made six years earlier. She had risked her job to share the wonders of Library with her Kindergarten class, and was delighted to find out later they excitedly had told their parents of the magical experience.

This encouraged others to explore Library. That reassured Sarah that the risks and resulting consequences had been worth it.

She recognized a couple of her former students, now grown into young adults. She acknowledged them with a smile and a brief wave as she silently maneuvered to a quite area where her confidant, Bjorn Esterday, sat researching facts for a story he was working on.

As she put her items down on the table, Bjorn said, "I'm glad you came, Sarah. It's nice being able to contact you now that you have a communication device."

Sarah smiled and whispered, "Well, it only took me a few years to earn enough credits to afford one."

She thought briefly about the interchange she'd had with Pip Courtly earlier regarding the new internship program and was determined to try and make the best of it for those students. Somehow.

Bjorn smiled and stood up to pull out a chair for Sarah. As she smiled back, her hand gently touched his hand. He leaned in to seat her and captured a brief whiff of her fragrant hair as the soft locks tossed lightly against his cheek. He shifted his chair to be close to hers and sat. Sarah glanced up at him shyly, then opened her book.

Sarah wondered why Bjorn never spoke about his past, about the gap between when they first met, and today when they had recently become re-acquainted. She wondered why he chose to shroud his past in mystery, downplay his accomplishments, and only speak of the future. Sarah smiled to herself and hoped she wasn't reading too much into it.

Sarah liked the idea of meeting Bjorn in Library because it forced her to move close to him, get right up to his ear and have an intimate conversation while sensing his cologne.

She leaned over to Bjorn quite cognizant of the fact that people were nearby. Softly, she whispered to Bjorn about her day.

Bjorn pulled back, his brow knitted as he looked straight at her and said quietly, "Sarah, you are a brilliant instructor and you are fetching coffee for some under-aged executive...as a temporary worker?"

Sarah thought he'd have been pleased that she was earning money and on target to get fully out of debt this summer.

"Well, better to be humble about it and responsibly pay my bills, don't you think? Or would you prefer I wallow in self-entitled pity, searching for somebody to blame and whine that I'm not solvent? That never got anything done. I am taking action to change my life...and keep a roof over my head, Bjorn. Can't you see that?"

"That's the perk? You get paid? And the opportunity to put up with a flirtatious,

53

underage comic-absorbed leech who doesn't have the ability to focus on completing a full sentence?" He rolled his eyes. "Sure thing, baby. You're living the dream," he snapped sarcastically and then redirected his attention back to the papers and books before him.

Bjorn paused and looked up again at Sarah's crestfallen expression. "I'm sorry. that was harsh. Here is what I mean to say. Comply with your contract so you can get out of debt. I understand that. We all have to pay our bills, but be careful that your boss doesn't push the limits of a professional employee-employer relationship, Sarah."

Sarah looked around and turned a page in her opened book and then looked at him, "Well, there are other perks. I can send 'deadmail' without waiting for the censors to redact a letter I write..."

"Not 'deadmail', you mean 'redmail' as in Redacted Electronic Document." He smiled, still in the mode to check the facts. "At The Daily Memo, we only wait one day before the censors clear us, so you mean to tell me that Courtly headquarters expedites redmail faster than a newspaper with deadlines?"

"Well, those Courtly execs get things done fast." She took his hand to distract him from the papers he started to focus on and leaned so close to him, she had to shut her eyes as she spoke into his neck, tickling it with her warm breath as she continued.

"The air conditioning works. The clocks on the walls are all set to the same time and run at the same speed. If my chair breaks, I get a new one fast. I have my own trash basket. I'm not rationed on pens, paper, paper clips and other supplies."

"Sarah," Bjorn interrupted as he leaned toward her, whispering. "You possess so much knowledge. You even know about those antique computers that used cables to talk to each other. You bond with all your students. When the Administrators tried to break you by swapping you from Kindergarten to High school, you transitioned and adapted. How are you using any of your skills on this temp corp job? How are you moving forward?" Bjorn pulled back to see her expression and awaited her response.

"Well," she said as she straightened out the books in front of her. She looked around and saw that perhaps she had spoke too loudly. She paused, then leaned into Bjorn and whispered, "Today I met one of the Courtly attorneys. His name is... um... Atsushi. I took a chance and told him a few things I can do, and he said arcane computer networking just may be something they could pay me extra for."

"What? They'd pay you for ancient tech?"

"Well, Pip's father, Skipper Courtly, is really the boss and he just bought this old structure. Been abandoned forever. He wants everything restored and that includes setting up a network like the old days, which hardly anybody knows how to do or cares to do these days."

"When are you supposed to have time for extra projects?" Bjorn muttered.

"I can do work after hours or on weekends."

Bjorn looked at her. "After hours?"

Sarah put both hands on her lap. "Look, Bjorn, if I can scrape together a little here and a little there, then by the end of the summer, I will be totally debt free and...that...might open up some new possibilities...for..."

"...For us?" Bjorn finished her sentence grinning. "So, you'll put up with a lecherous boss and help indoctrinate high school kids into thinking that being an indentured servant is really helpful to their futures..."

"It's just for a little while, Bjorn," Sarah murmured quietly, "Just the summer..."

"All to buy your freedom?" Bjorn sarcastically added.

Sarah persisted, "I can structure the program for the students so they do get something out of it. I can make a difference that way…"

Bjorn smiled and kissed her lightly on the cheek, "You always cared about your students."

"Like you care about your stories…" She smiled, her cheek still tingling from his light touch.

Bjorn took a deep breath.

"I'm sorry for being so judgmental, Sarah. I know we don't always have a choice over what jobs we do and just need to do the best we can in the circumstances…" He paused, then continued, "So, I knew you'd understand."

"I'm sorry, did we switch gears or am I missing something?" Sarah smiled

58

grasping his hand tightly, urging him to clarify.

"I may as well just..." He went silent.

"Come on, Bjorn. I always confide in you. You can tell me. What's on your mind?"

"OK. OK," he took another deep breath as he focused. "You remember Sammy, right? My editor? Well, he's been ordered to downsize Investigative Reporting."

"What?" Sarah's eyes opened wide as she realized she spoke rather loudly and was responded to with hushes and disapproving looks. She lowered her voice to a whisper, "What does that mean for you, Bjorn?"

"Sammy Scribe had to get rid of some good people, but some of us could transfer to other departments. We held a lottery for the people who could transfer and I lost. I got to pick last so there was only one spot left and it was in Lifestyles." He looked away, ashamed.

Sarah gazed into his eyes earnestly, "This economy is like quicksand. You never know when your secure footing will vanish. Oh, Bjorn, I am so sorry, but at least you still have income...you still have a job."

"Yeah. I'm trying to look at the bright side." He forced a grin.

"Well, here is one good thing. I won't have to worry about you going out on one of those AnCor assignments anymore. So many reporters have died covering the wars. When I met you six years ago at the train station, I was certain I'd see you again, but then years went by and I never heard from you."

"I replayed that moment in my head over and over, Sarah. You know, I did go to your elementary school the week after we met, but they said you didn't work there anymore and didn't know where you had gone. So, when Investigative Reporting asked me to join them and take on a war assignment... I took it. I didn't think I'd be out in the middle of nowhere for five years straight. I didn't think I had anybody back home waiting for me or even missing me."

"Well, I'm glad you looked me up when you got back, Bjorn. Really glad." Sarah smiled. "And covering Lifestyle stories, I know you'll be safe."

"Yeah. OK," he said half-heartedly agreeing. "Sammy said facts and hard news was out. Gossip, décor, and makeovers are in." he shrugged.

Sarah leaned over to hug Bjorn.

"Oh, I wish I could make it better somehow..." Sarah soothed.

"Actually, you can, Sarah. I mean if your offer is sincere." He looked at her.

"Of course I'm serious," she said.

"Now that you are close to Pip and Skipper Courtly...could you..." He paused.

"Yes?" She asked, "How can my one-day-old tenuous connections at my temporary summer job help you?"

12 CHAPTER Year 2036: Intern Tour (Continuous Ch 24)

Huge bay doors slammed shut after the truck backed in with a load of Courtly Dynamics Corporation mail.

Here, on a remote edge of the Courtly campus, was the old mail distribution center, which survived annual demolition orders that were never enforced, but merely piled up on some bureaucrat's desk.

This neglected and almost forgotten structure was overrun with native wild flowers and climbing ivy. Nearby was a barn where spare horses were kept to use in the event of an Anti-Corporate Activity alert.

Practiced workers grabbed sacks and boxes. They fed the mail through scanning machines, which sorted the items into different piles. Flying drones scurried to pick up and deliver pre-sorted piles to final destinations.

Outside this building, on the outer wall, was a worn carved frieze. Once painted, the faded colors were now barely visible. Foliage partially blocked the old sign. It was the streamlined image of an eagle, beak pointing to the right, wings up as if it were about to embark on a flight. Under the bird, was a squared off ring of nine stars, once probably painted gold, but now worn away to a stony white. Arched around the top of the eagle were the words, "United States Postal Service".

Nearby was another smaller logo in a circle. Also facing right, this image was of a man on a galloping horse. His blue jacket evoked images of an old fashioned "pony express". Brown paint, still visible, colored the mail pouch behind the rider's saddle.

The sounds of robots, workers, and flying drones echoed against the cement floors.

Sarah looked into the young fresh faces of students now showing up for their first day of privileged mandatory unpaid work hours. These students had come from near and far, accepting their fate.

Sarah smiled, welcoming them, quietly understanding their hope that this would someday lead to an income. Sometimes circumstances force a person to cross over to the corporate world. She deliberately had taken on the responsibility to make these malleable souls reap some educational benefits even as they sweltered for three hot months without pay.

The crowd of students wore loosely fitting identical smocks with Courtly corp logos. One quiet 21 year old boy wore the practical garb of the Earth Farmer under his smock. He stood there silent, fiddling with his name tag, which read "Joshua", while keeping his eyes downcast.

Sarah addressed the young interns. "You've all had time to meet each other. This is the mail room. In 1775, a man named Benjamin Franklin was appointed the first postmaster general for the United States Postal Service. In 1833, in Illinois, Abraham Lincoln became the postmaster general at age 24. At the beginning of the 2000's the Post Office turned a profit of nearly a billion dollars a year, delivering billions of printed papers and packages to nearly 151 million addresses annually..." Sarah took a breath.

"What are dollars?" one student asked.

"It was the name of the money used before credits," Sarah smiled. She paused briefly then continued, "OK. So, the congress of that time wanted all government services to be privatized, so it demanded more money than the Post Office had in its accounts, and the Post Office was forced to go bankrupt. Immediately, Skipper Courtly's grandfather bought it all including buildings, operations, everything, along with similar city enterprises, in an auction. This structure here he turned into the Courtly mail center, servicing the entire Courtly territory today. It is in this building that you will start your apprenticeships."

Another intern called out, "Was this the pre office? I heard my grandma talking about a pre office."

"Didn't you have to buy membership in a mail club to be allowed to get packages and stuff?" a third asked. "Like we do today?"

Sarah could see more students beginning to interrupt, anxiously waving hands with other questions. She held up her palm. "One at a time , please. First, the short name used for United States Postal Service was Post Office, not the pre office, but," she smiled reassuringly, "that was close!"

"What happened to the pre office?" another piped in.

Sarah addressed the entire group. "Well, as I said, a while ago, the Post Office was a nationwide network of delivery channels, using boats, wheeled vehicles, horses, and airborne transportation to bring mail to every citizen. Rich and poor."

Sarah smiled at the apprentices, "They didn't need mail clubs back then. The operation was supported by the revenue raised from the sale of tiny adhesive pictures called 'stamps', because they were not supported by tax-payer money."

"So the congress was doing this to all the government services back then?" another intern asked.

"When the law makers targeted the Post Office, they made the Post Office pay billions of dollars to the government. This had never been done before."

One intern interrupted, "What do you mean? Didn't they pay a little each year?"

Sarah patiently replied, "No. They had a payment schedule spreading the payments over fifty years, but the law makers changed the schedule to make them pay it off in ten years. No other department or business had ever been made to pay a fifty-year schedule so fast."

Curious, several interns were whispering with each other until one piped up with, "What happened?"

Sarah explained, "When the Post Office surprised everyone by making enough money from the sale of the stamps to pay off the debt, the Legislature said 'No. We will not let you pay off the debt we imposed on you.' This law was known as the PAEA or Postal Accountability Enhancement Act. This law said they would never accept Post Office money resulting from the sale of stamps."

"I wonder if the workers at the pre office got mad at the people who voted for this PAEA thing," another intern blurted out.

"Good point. Well, in this law," Sarah responded, "they also said no record could be made showing how each law maker voted, that's why the people couldn't find out which one of them voted to dismantle the Post Office. So, the Post Office died, and the buildings went up for auction and that's when Skipper Courtly's grandfather bought it up."

Sarah took a breath to change the subject, "After you have worked here for a couple of weeks in the mail center, your skill set will be evaluated to determine what other talents you can offer other departments during your work time, here. Are there any more questions before we continue the tour of Courtly campus?"

In the back of the crowd, one apprentice raised his hand. "At the end of our internship, when school starts up again, will you, Miss Paradise, still be our contact?"

Sarah smiled kindly at the nervous youth. She peered at his name tag and then replied, "Well, Mykel, that's a good point to bring up. No. I will resume my regular teaching assignment just as you will be resuming your school schedule. Then, when you graduate, you will return here for three years. I don't think I will be here, then, but I'm sure they will find you a new contact. I'm only working at Courtly for the summer."

Sarah looked around at the other students. "Are there any other questions? Demetri? Maria? Victor? Li? Hong? Carina? Alexandra? Anyone?" Sarah took a breath and motioned them to follow her to the next stop on their tour.

As she pivoted away from the group to lead them, a shy Earth Farmer boy cleared his throat and, nervously asked, "About a decade ago, Courtly Dynamics Corporation executives signed a treaty with our elders."

"I don't...," Sarah peered at his name

tag, "...Joshua. I'm not familiar with any Courtly business deals..."

Joshua continued to explain, "Earth Farmers till the land to grow food. Courtly protects our produce and livestock in exchange for a portion of our crops."

From the back of the group, another intern, Alexandra, touched his shoulder, whispering, "That's enough. Shhhh," and then melted back into the rear of the crowd.

"Well, that's all right. He can continue." Sarah smiled at the 18 year old girl, who immediately looked at her own feet, avoiding the eyes of Miss Paradise. Sarah urged the young Earth Farmer on, "Please continue, Joshua."

"Our land is being destroyed. In some areas the soil smokes. One of our farmers died when he inhaled the smoke."

One of the other interns groaned,

saying, "Oh, not this again. Your people are always doing this trying to fight progress. We need pollution to improve our environment."

Another joined in, "That's propaganda. You can still progress and invent without damaging our food supply. Joshua has a point."

"All right, class. Settle down," Sarah refereed. "Is that what you wanted to say, Joshua?" Sarah asked the youth.

"No. I have more. The acres of soil we can NOT farm on is increasing. Courtly Dynamics Corporation still expects an annual increased yield, but they are the ones damaging our land."

"What's your point?" groaned the first intern.

"I want to know when Courtly will fulfill their responsibility and fix the damage they've done so we can continue our food production agreement." Joshua finished, almost surprised at his own bold demeanor and suddenly reverted to his shy neutral self, with eyes downcast. Now, his cheeks burned red as if flabbergasted that he had just spoken the way he did.

"Um. Well. Hmm. I don't know the answer to that one. As I said, this is a summer job for me, also," Sarah shrugged.

"All right, class." Sarah continued cheerfully, "Now that we all are better acquainted with each other, let's move on to our next stop on the tour." Sarah started to move along and the interns followed her.

Over her shoulder, she continued to speak, "I am your point of contact during the summer. I will be checking in with you regularly to gauge your progress and development. But, I won't know all the answers."

Sarah stopped. Then turned to face the little group, "But I will try my best to find out answers for you... or tell you with whom you may speak to find those answers."

She smiled reassuringly, then, just as quickly, she announced, "Next stop is the break room. This way... Let's see if we can find an executive who could answer Joshua's question, shall we, class?"

13 CHAPTER Year 2036: Castle (Continuous Ch 25)

The castle exterior, littered with cobwebs and bird nests, overlooked a small pristine lake. Old stone window ledges cast long shadows on the overgrown weeds. Trees, in need of trimming, loomed up as tangled remnants of a bygone, well-manicured era.

Although the castle was dilapidated, untamed vegetation on the shores of the lapping lake brought a rugged beauty to the lands.

The expansive mansion was a blend of old rustic architecture and modern conveniences. The building had been erected less than 50 years earlier, but it was designed to look much older.

Along the winding driveway, leading to the massive front doors, stood several weathered "for sale" signs stuck haphazardly into the ground. As he approached the house, Skipper Courtly pulled up each "for sale" sign, tucking them under his arm as he walked.

This building had been vacant for some time. A force field surrounded the perimeter of the building to prevent squatters from getting in. Most real estate agents used such a force field to protect vacant homes in between showings.

A thick layer of dry leaves crunched with every step Skipper took as he ascended the broad stairs to the front door. At the top of the steps, he triumphantly tossed away all his gathered "for sale" signs.

Skipper then marched up to the front

of the massive structure and placed his hand on a nearby plate. He waited. The force field dropped.

"Glad they got my handprint programming in so quickly so that it responds to my touch." Skipper smiled to his son, Pip. "Nobody can enter now without my permission."

Skipper was indeed the new owner. It had been sold. Yes. To him.

The ornate doors creaked opened on old fashioned hinges and both father and son slowly walked into the dark dank-smelling foyer. Dry leaves from outside fluttered in before the heavy door slammed behind them.

Skipper smiled and clasped his hands together as if finally he had gotten that gift he had been waiting for. By contrast, Pip groaned as he calculated all the costs of remodeling. Pip leaned up against the wall only to have a dusty cob-webbed sconce above his head clatter to the ground, barely missing him.

The clatter made Skipper spin around, "Isn't this fantastic?"

"Sure, Dad. Just what YOU wanted. But, have you considered how much it will cost to fix this place up?"

"Don't be ridiculous, Pip. We are Courtlys. That means the people will be honored to work for us gratis."

"Dad, it seems really extravagant and a little spooky. We don't have the money for this sort of indulgence. Where is the money coming from? Didn't Uncle Jack used to say we shouldn't spend our money on..."

"Pip Courtly! Money, money, money! Stop obsessing about money! Your Uncle Jack is dead. His whole family is dead. Gone. I don't want to hear you quote him anymore. It's irritating. Get it through your head that the people need to be reassured that the Courtly family is firmly in power... and money buys power."

"What are you trying to prove, Dad? We are already the largest corporation in this region. What more do we need?"

"It's never ever enough. Don't you understand? You grow by stretching.

79

And the Courtly family has never had a castle before. We need a castle to be a proper kingdom." Skipper spun about with large swooping arm gestures to make his point more animated.

"Dad. This place isn't from a kingdom. It's got no history. It's just a big old broken down house."

Skipper spun sharply to face Pip, shocked that his own son would say such a thing. Slowly, Skipper explained with exaggerated deliberation, "Its legend says a spirit of ultimate power haunts the dungeon. I will figure out what that spook wants. I will master the power the ghost has, then I will master all other corporations everywhere. They will all surrender to me."

"That's a lot of 'I's," Pip started, then suddenly he became aware of his father's intentions. "Wait. You want to get rid of the other corporations? But who would we trade with if they were gone?"

"Don't be impertinent, Pip."

Impatiently, Skipper hurried toward the rear wall and disappeared into a dark hallway to begin descending a small moss-covered stone staircase. Each step became more narrow and slippery.

Pip followed.

"Dad. You just sound ...I don't know... If this is really where you want to live, I'm gonna keep my place in the city, if you don't mind."

Skipper tried to pull open a heavy door at the base of the stairs, fighting the ravages of rust and wear. The hinges stuck. Nearby on a hook was an old fashioned key. Skipper grabbed it to unlock the door, then tugged again. Age had collected into all the crevices of the wooden door, nearly sealing it. Finally, with one hearty yank, the door yielded.

There were no windows in this room. It was the basement. Unevenly shaped stone blocks made up the walls. Skipper reached for an old switch on the wall. Lights dimly flickered. The room revealed shadowy contours of cluttered wooden statues and objects that looked as if they had been carelessly tossed out of a large dump truck.

81

When the two Courtly men stepped inside the room, their eyes tried to adjust. They peered up the wall to the high shadowed ceiling above. About four feet below the ceiling, they could make out a ledge extending roughly two feet from the wall. Perhaps this sturdy ledge once held the heavy statues which now were scattered about on the basement stone floor.

"What would people do down here?" Pip whispered as he looked around. Suddenly, his eye caught an object in the center of the cluttered heap.

Inside one alcove was a solitary coffin, standing on end amidst the rubble.

"Oh. There it is," Skipper excitedly explained, "You see this? The last owner was a collector and he left his entire art collection here because of the legend."

"And what's that creepy coffin for?"

"The fable says one must stay in the room all night to see the ghost."

"Superstition."

"Superstition? Pip Courtly? I tell you

when I first came in here, this collection was all lined up neatly the day I made an offer on this place. The very next day, when everything was locked down and secure so no intruders could get inside, this mess happened."

"So, some disgruntled previous owners trashed it?"

Frustrated, Skipper clarified, "No. The legend! These supernatural powers emanate from this room."

"Dad, you're acting like YOU will capture those powers..." Pip laughed with his mouth wide opened as he adjusted his glasses.

"Oh, I will soon possess those powers," a determined Skipper replied. "If I can prevail against this haunting spirit, I will beat anything and anyone that tries to come up against me."

Skipper angrily stormed back up the stairs leaving a trail of damp footprints as he walked. Pip quickly followed behind. Skipper passed through the foyer and then entered an ornate room.

A throne room.

"Why does this room look so... clean? And so fancy!" Pip asked as he looked around. He eyes focused on the imposing throne set up on a stately raised platform.

Eight burgundy-red velvet-covered marble steps led up to the throne itself. The garishly ornate golden throne dominated the entire room. Large new red velvet cushions had been placed carefully at the base of the platform.

"Terms of the sale, my son. Terms of the sale. I will be receiving guests during the remodel, so I wanted this room done first." Pip looked around. The room was baroque in décor, extravagantly adorned with ornate filigree and florid convoluted gold accents. The huge elevated throne made Pip feel like a preschooler. He remembered the days when a story teller would ease into a big chair and direct him and all his classmates to sit on the floor so she could read aloud to them. For some reason the recollection made Pip feel uncomfortable. He shook off memories of his childhood, wondering how he might now take over this space for his own use.

"Well," Pip conceded, "I guess it could be a good place for a party..."

Pip's thought was interrupted by a loud reverberating gong, making him trip backwards and fall into the pile of throw pillows.

Instantly, Skipper Courtly, knowing exactly what that sound was, jumped up and rushed to the front door.

Recovering, Pip scrambled to his feet shooting slippery throw pillows out against the slick polished floors. Pip caught up with his father and found him struggling to open the huge front door.

Pip helped by tugging on the massive iron handles. Finally, slowly, the door creaked open.

"Welcome. Come in, come in. No need to dawdle! Inside, my man." Skipper waved the visitor in. A gust of wind blew dry leaves into the foyer before he could close the door behind his guest.

"Thank you, Mr. Courtly. I'm Bjorn

Esterday. My newspaper 'The Daily Memo', sent me to start a series of articles on your remodeling project, as you requested, sir," Bjorn politely stated as he looked around the foyer.

The Lifestyles reporter stepped on dry leaves which cracked into dust on the floor beneath his feet.

"Yes. Yes. Yes. It's just us here. No staff. Not yet. Oh!" Skipper Courtly paused as he beckoned Bjorn to follow him down the hallway.

"Mr. Esterday, I do have a humble little room all set up where we can chat. It's very cozy. Oh, yes, and this is my son, Pip. This way..."

Skipper sprinted ahead of Pip and Bjorn to climb up onto the throne first, slipping on only one velvet cushion before catching his balance. He eased himself into its plush upholstery. Slowly, his palms traced the arms on this all-encompassing chair. Skipper showed his delight with a smile.

Silently, he caught the confused look of Bjorn and ignored the eye rolling of Pip, who simply leaned back against a wall, crossing his arms with a smirk.

Skipper gestured to the cushions below on the floor and said, "Please, Mr. Esterday, take a seat."

Bjorn scanned the room for a chair, realized there were no other options besides the cushions piled at the base of the throne. He slowly eased himself down onto a cushion and assumed a cross-legged position, trying to remain poker-faced.

Pip, now amused, crossed over to deliberately place himself on the steps half way between his father, Skipper, on the throne above, and Bjorn, sitting on the scattered pillows below.

Skipper leaned forward with anticipation awaiting Bjorn's first question.

14 CHAPTER- What will happen next?

Ace puts the game away into Jack's briefcase. and wonders vaguely if players can become addicted to the electronic entertainment device.

Since Queenie Courtly is fond of the quilt designs made by Earth Farmer wife Ruth Lantz, Jack decides to arrange a nice dinner for the entire Earth Farmer family as a thank you for minding Ace along with their family.

As Ruth and Queenie walk together toward the train's dining car, they are unaware that the AnCors have already boarded the train. Will they notice?

Why are the AnCors after the Courtly family?

A few years later, in 2036, we see that Courtly City is ruled by a new executive, which is Jack's brother Skipper.

Skipper wants to remodel a property by the lake into a castle just for him to remind everybody that he is in charge, now.

Sarah Paradise needs to augment her teaching salary by taking on a temporary Summer job at the Courtly Headquarters. She works for Pip Courtly, Skipper's Son, and will give the student interns tours of the Courtly Headquarters.

FACT: The PAEA is the Postal Accountability Enhancement Act.

ജ To Be Continued... ○ভ

Wynter Sommers

15 Did You Know

In the 1990's video game rehabs started, but today, with the increase of interactive virtual reality games, more and more people are using gaming as a way to avoid dealing with their real-life problems.

Something becomes an "addiction" when it negatively monopolizes so much of your time that you neglect your obligations in other areas of your life. It is any habit you've developed that interferes with healthy human interactions.

In a general rehabilitation program which addresses addiction to games, rehab therapy will include removing the game from the patient for 30 days and provide therapy to the patient to teach the individual how to cope with the real-world problem they are trying to avoid.

Partial List of Bankruptcies filed or were filed and then dismissed by the courts

<u>Municipal Bankruptcy</u> Filings: 61 (Includes one municipality with two separate bankruptcy filings). This includes water districts, hospital authorities and other municipal units.

<u>General-Local Government Bankruptcy Filings</u>:
- ✓ Stockton, California
- ✓ San Bernardino, California
- ✓ Mammoth Lakes, Calf. (Dismissed)
- ✓ Vallejo, California
- ✓ Desert Hot Springs, California
- ✓ Detroit, Michigan
- ✓ Bridgeport, Connecticut
- ✓ Harrisburg, Pennsylvania
- ✓ Prichard, Alabama (1999 and 2009)
- ✓ Jefferson County, Alabama
- ✓ Central Falls, Rhode Island
- ✓ Harrisburg, Pennsylvania. (Dismissed)
- ✓ Boise County, Idaho (Dismissed)

ABOUT Wynter Sommers

Wynter Sommers is the pseudonym for an American writing team, which harnesses multiple skills in technology, research, and education. Formally trained with a PhD in Education, Wynter Sommers blends academic classroom experience, with corporate sophistication, and a passion for developing more effective student insights.

Wynter Sommers has taught classrooms of enthusiastic children. She has a heart to inspire creativity and develop critical thinking skills, all to encourage students to make wise choices in life. She wants to impart the talent of honing one's skills in self-reliance and collaborative team work. Despite any environmental barriers outside of an individual's control, Wynter Sommers wishes to impart the message that genuine hope, love, and peace can help us overcome obstacles, and cement friendships. Wynter Sommers hopes you enjoy the other *Bjorn Esterday Was not Born Yesterday* stories in this series.